An Introduction to the
Differential Calculus
By Means of Finite Differences

MAXWELL PRESS

An Introduction to the
Differential Calculus
By Means of Finite Differences

Roberdeau Buchanan S.B.,

Assistant in the Nautical Almanac Office,
U.S. Naval Observatory,
Author of the Mathematical Theory of Eclipses,
Treatise on the Projection of the Sphere, Etc.,

MAXWELL PRESS

Chennai   Trichy   New Delhi

MAXWELL PRESS

This edition has been published in india by arrangement with Carson Books, UK

ISBN 978-93-91270-00-1   Maxwell Press

All rights reserved   No. 44, Nallathambi Street,
Printed and bound in India   Triplicane, Chennai 600 005

MJP   1146   © Publishers, 2023

Publisher :   C. Janarthanan

Publisher's Note

The legacy of a country is in its varied cultural heritage, historical literature, developments in the field of economy and science. The top nations in the world are competing in the field of science, economy and literature. This vast legacy has to be conserved and documented so that it can be bestowed to the future generation. The knowledge of this legacy is slowly getting perished in the present generation due to lack of documentation.

Keeping this in mind, the concern with retrospective acquiring of rare books has been accented recently by the burgeoning reprint industry. Maxwell Press is gratified to retrieve the rare collections with a view to bring back those books that were landmarks in their time.

In this effort, a series of rare books would be republished under the banner, "Maxwell Press". The books in the reprint series have been carefully selected for their contemporary usefulness as well as their historical importance within the intellectual. We reconstruct the book with slight enhancements made for better presentation, without affecting the contents of the original edition.

Most of the works selected for republishing covers a huge range of subjects, from history to anthropology. We believe this reprint edition will be a service to the numerous researchers and practitioners active in this fascinating field. We allow readers to experience the wonder of peering into a scholarly work of the highest order and seminal significance.

MAXWELL PRESS

PREFACE.

AN INTRODUCTION TO THE DIFFERENTIAL CALCULUS, BY MEANS OF FINITE DIFFERENCES.

BY ROBERDEAU BUCHANAN, S. B.

From the time the author commenced the study of the Calculus he has been of the opinion that an introductory text-book was a want to be supplied. And Finite Differences undoubtedly offer the best method of explanation. All that the student is required to know at first, is mere differencing which is easily understood. In article 19 and those following, formulae from Finite Differences are given, but not their derivation, and the student can regard them and use them simply as algebraic equations. They constitute the proof of this method of explaining the Calculus and the student may omit them until he advances further in the study.

Professor Newcomb says in the Preface to his Algebra "that all mathematical conceptions require time to become engrafted upon the mind, and the more time, the more their abstruseness." And again in the same work, "one well known principle underlying the acquisition of all knowledge is that an idea cannot be fully grasped by the youthful mind, unless it is presented in some concrete form. Whenever possible an abstract idea must be embodied in some visible representation."

For the first reason, the author has presented the first example several times, varying the questions each time; and for the second reason has explained the example in more than one way—by means of numbers, by Finite Differences, by an algebraic equation, by a differential equation, and by geometrical representation; all converging to the same end, that the student may see the similarity between them all and thus gain his idea of a differential, and also of the first principles of the calculus. It is the purpose of the author to give only the elementary idea leaving the rest to the student's instructor.

Since reading Professor Bledsoe's *Philosophy of Mathematics*, some years ago, the author has not been satisfied with the explanations usually given of the calculus which make a finite difference become a differential by suppressing certain terms; whereas a finite difference cannot become a differential except by a change of value to which these suppressed terms contribute. The author does not wish to be understood as denying the truths of the Calculus, but suggests that a better method of explanation might be adopted. Nor does he wish to hurt the feelings of writers on the calculus; and for that reason has refrained from quoting the works of any living author. It is the method of explanation which he controverts, which seems to have been almost unanimously adopted by writers since the time of Euler in 1787, and perhaps earlier. THE AUTHOR.

2015 Q Street, Washington, D. C.
1905, February 27.

Then, h being infinitely small compared with $2x$ can be neglected. Others say that here h may undergo any change of value without affecting x, so letting h diminish until it is zero we have equation (5) as given above.*

In Davis and Peck's *Dictionary of Mathematics*, Article *Infinitesimal*, this principle is very broadly stated.

"When several quantities either finite or infinitesimal are connected together by the signs plus and minus, all except those of the lowest order may be neglected without affecting the value of the expression. Thus

$$\text{or} \quad \left.\begin{array}{l} a + dx + dx^2 = a \\ dx + dx^2 + dx^3 = dx \text{ "} \end{array}\right\} \quad (8)$$

2. Professor Bledsoe in his *Philosophy of Mathemics*† attacks this method of explanation, because in Equation 7, h is supposed to be equal to zero on one side of the equation but retained as a small finite quantity on the other. And also in equations (8) asks, Can the first one be exactly equal to a? (p. 64) And also "No one can look the principle fairly and fully in the face, that an infinitely small quantity may be subtracted from a finite quantity, without making even an infinitely small difference in its value, and yet regard it otherwise than absurd" (ibid p. 63) Professor Bledsoe states that this method is sanctioned by such names as Roberval, Pascal, Leibnitz, the Marquis de L'Hopital and others, and yet it is apt to inspire the student, that the calculus is "merely a method of approximation." (pp. 65, 70).

DeMorgan, a great name in mathematics has evidently himself seen the objections to this method and gives a long explanation of a limit (which however he makes no further use of); then steps over the difficulty by giving a number of differentials "without demonstrating them, therefor, or even defining them."‡

Newton, one of the discoverers of the calculus conceived a line to be made by the motion of a point, its path, in fact; hence the names he adopts—fluents and fluxions.

Professors Rice and Johnson of the United States Naval Academy have published a calculus founded on the idea of rates and velocities, etc. The works of these three latter writers are not open to the objections which have been made to the method by limits.

3. *Author's explanation by means of Finite Differences.* On

* James Haddon Examples and Solutions in the Differential Calculus. Weale's Series.

† Published by J. B. Lippincott & Co., Philadelphia 1874, p. 212.

‡ De Morgan Differential Calculus, London 1842; chapter *i*.

account of their analogy, one to the other, Finite Differences seem to be the natural explanation to the Calculus, when their diversity is also pointed out. This method is more general than those mentioned in the foregoing pages. Moreover it easily explains and verifies the objection raised by Professor Bledsoe.

It will be sufficient for our purpose at present to assume as a general equation, the following:

$$u = a + (b + cx)^2 \qquad (9)$$

First, let $a = 0$ $b = 0$ and $c = 1$ which gives the equation (1) of Article 1.

$$u = x^2 \qquad (10)$$

Now assume successive values of x, the independent variable, positive and negative and find the resulting values of u. Place the values of x in column 1, Example 1, and the resulting values

EXAMPLE 1, EQUATION 10. $u = x^2$

Col. 1.	Col. 2.	Col. 3.	Col. 4.	Col. 5.
x	u	Δ_1	Δ_2	Δ_3
−5	+25			
		−9		
4	16		+2	
		7		0
3	9		2	
		5		0
2	4		2	
		3		0
−1	+1		2	
		−1		0
0	0		2	
		+1		0
+1	+1		2	
		3		0
2	4		2	
		5		0
3	9		2	
		7		0
4	16		2	
		9		0
5	25		+2	
		+11		
+6	+36			

of u in column 2, which is headed u. The proper signs of the quantities should be carefully considered and written whenever a sign changes. Next, form the column of First Differences, Δ_1,* (column 3) by subtracting algebraically each number from the number below it, in column 2 and placing the difference below the line, that is, 0 opposite the space between the two numbers. It will be seen presently that this position for the difference is the

---

* The character Δ in the Calculus of Finite Differences is a symbol of operation as d is in the Differential Calculus, it is often however taken to represent the Differences themselves; in the following examples it has this latter meaning.

correct place, and it is important that it should be so placed.* This column is headed Δ_1, the usual designation for a *first differ- ence.* Next in like manner form the column of *Second Differences* Δ_2 (column 4) subtracting algebraically as before, each number in column 3 from the one below it, and placing the difference on the line, that is, opposite the space between the two. This is the proper position for the second difference. This column is headed Δ_2 and in the present example is a constant 2. There are no Third Differences Δ_3 in this example since if we try to subtract our re- sults equal zero and moreover all the higher differences must be zero also. The second differences being a constant are independent of the value of the function u.

4. The reader will now have but little difficulty in understand- ing the meanings of differential, and differential coefficient:

The differences of the values of x column 1 which are all unity are *practically dx* the differential of *x;* and the numbers column 3, the First Differences, are *practically* the first differential co- efficient of the values of u in column 2, depending upon the values of x, column 1. And the Second Differences column 4 are *practically* the second differential coefficient of u. These numbers show the analogy of differences and differentials. The word *practically* used above alludes to their diversity which will be considered presently.

To show these statements, resume equation (10)

$$\left. \begin{array}{l} u = x^2 \\[2mm] \text{Differentiate} \quad \dfrac{du}{dx} = 2x \end{array} \right\} \qquad (11)$$

This equation will *practically,* that is very nearly, give the numbers in column 3, the First Differences. But first an im- portant distinction between a difference and a differential must be stated. The value $+5$ is the first difference belonging to the value of $u = +4$ or x = 2 and properly is placed *below* the line. The differential coefficient of x $= +2$, and $u = +4$ would prop- erly stand *on* the line with u, so that its value would be between 3 and 5. Now by equation (11) compute various values of $\dfrac{du}{dx}$ and compare them with the example. They are, in equations of the second degree, correctly speaking, the means of the two differences above and below the line, thus:

---

* In works on Finite Differences the line of Differences is usually placed on the line of the primitive; or else the values of the function are placed on a line with the differences in columns below. The method described in the text is the more general and seems to possess more advantages than any other.

$$\text{If } x = -4 \qquad \frac{du}{dx} = 2x = -8 \quad \text{on the line}$$

$$x = -1 \qquad \frac{du}{dx} = 2x = -2 \quad \text{on the line}$$

$$x = +2 \qquad \frac{du}{dx} = 2x = +4 \quad \text{on the line}$$

$$x = +2.5 \quad \textit{below the line} \qquad \frac{du}{dx} = 2x = +5 \cdot \quad \textit{below the line}$$

It should be remarked that for so low an order as the square the differentials and differences agree with one another more closely than they do in the higher powers, which will be shown by an equation of the fifth power on a subsequent page.

Resume equation (4) of Article 1.

$$u_1 - u = 2xh + h^2$$

in which h is the increment of x and is always taken as unity in Finite Differences. It is also so taken in Example 1, column 1. Hence we have

$$u_1 - u = 2x + 1 \qquad\qquad (12)$$

from which we can compute the first differences, remembering that they fall below the line, and we have as follows:

$$\text{If } x = -4, \quad u_1 - u = 2x + 1 = -8 + 1 = -7$$
$$x = -1, \quad u_1 - u = 2x + 1 = -2 + 1 = -1$$
$$x = +2, \quad u_1 - u = 2x + 1 = +4 + 1 = +5$$
$$x = +2.5, \quad u_1 - u = 2x + 1 = +5 + 1 = +6$$

The last value $+6$ should fall half a line below the position of $x = 2.5$ which brings it upon the line below. We see here that universally for any given value of x the differences and differentials have not the same values.

Differentiate equation (11) a second time

$$\frac{d^2 u}{dx^2} = +2$$

a constant which is the value in Example 1, column 4 of the finite differences.

5. *Statement of the objections to the usual Method by Limits.* Equation (4) is a correct equation in Finite Differences provided h is a constant, usually taken as unity. With this value the equation gives

$$u_1 - u = 2x + 1$$

But as, Equa. (11) $\qquad \dfrac{du}{dx} = 2x$

We have $\qquad \dfrac{du}{dx} \cdot = (u_1 - u) - 1$

from which the differential coefficient of equation (10) may be computed from the finite differences, as we have shown above. We see also that to form the differential coefficient the quantity

h^2 or unity disappears by numerical subtraction merging into the term $(u_1 - u)$. By the method of limits this quantity h is divided

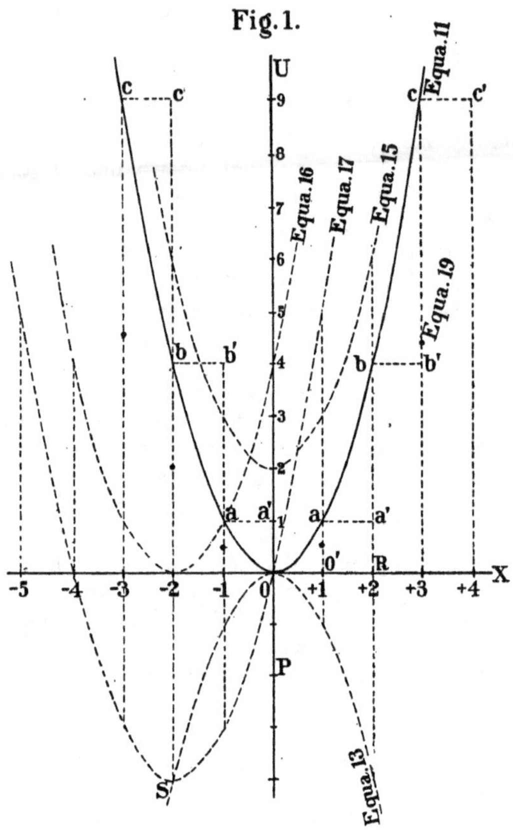

Fig. 1.

out in order to get rid of it as a factor to $2x$ giving the equation 7 as follows:

Equation 7,
$$\frac{u_1 - u}{h} = 2x + h$$

in which h in the second member decreases until it disappears while in the first member it is retained as an infinitely small quantity then called dx. This is by far the most unmathematical feature of this method. There is also another point. The equivalent of

$$\frac{du}{dx} \quad \text{is not} \quad \frac{u_1 - u}{h}, \quad \text{but;} \quad u_1 - u$$

Another objection noticed, is that equation (7) above given, is a correct equation in Finite Differences if h is taken equal to unity, which gives

$$u_1 - u = 2x + 1$$

but it would hardly be suitable to let this term decrease until we have $1 = 0$! so the notation h is substituted. This constant unity is the foundation of the theory of Finite Differences. With the quantity h, the above equation becomes equivocal. When h is unity or finite the equation is one of Finite Differences; but when h is infinitely small or zero it is supposed to be a differential equation.

The doctrine of limits cannot in this manner be applied to an equation of Finite Differences in which the whole essence and life of the equation depends upon this quantity h being a *constant* and a *finite* quantity. In order to find the differential coefficient from the finite difference this method makes the constant h disappear by division; the author's method on the other hand makes it disappear by subtraction which leaves the *absolute zero*. This subject will be still further examined on a subsequent page.

II.

6. *Graphical Representation.*   In Fig. 1 draw the axis of X a horizontal line, and the axis of U perpendicular to it at the point O.   Lay off the negative values of x on the left and the positive on the right.   The spaces between these points are each dx which is taken as unity in the example column 1.   Upon these points erect the ordinates and lay off the values of u resulting from the values of x in example 1.   These latter points a b c etc. may be connected by a curve which represents the equation 10 or 11.

7. If from the points a b c, etc., already found we draw the horizontal lines aa', bb', cc', etc., to the next ordinate on the right side (which is the positive direction of the motion of x, from left to right,) the lines o'a a'b b'c, etc., are the finite differences, belonging to the values of u.   These lines form a familiar figure in most works on the calculus, but which is usually not sufficiently explained, beyond a mere statement.   The angles which the chords Oa ab bc, etc., make with the axis of X are expressed by the tangents

$$\frac{ao'}{o'O} \quad , \quad \frac{ba'}{a'a} \quad \frac{cb'}{b'b} \quad , \quad \text{etc.} = \frac{\triangle u}{\triangle x}$$

which are very nearly the tangents to the middle points of the curve; but not exactly because the curvature is different at the two ends of the chords.   The differential coefficient for an ordinate midway between those in the figure takes account of the curvature, and gives the tangents to these middle points.   It will be noticed that on the left of the axis of U, du is laid off downwards, or in a negative direction, so that the tangent is a negative quantity, showing that the curve is moving in the negative direction, or downwards, in the figure.   And $\frac{d^2u}{dx^2}$ is positive; which also shows that the curve is convex towards the axis of X, Fig. 1.

8. If in Equation (10) we give the negative sign to the right member

$$u = -x^2 \tag{13}$$

we have

$$\left.\begin{aligned}\frac{du}{dx} &= -2x \\ \frac{d^2u}{dx^2} &= -2\end{aligned}\right\} \tag{14}$$

Which is shown as follows,

EXAMPLE 1, biz:

x	u	Δ_1	Δ_2
−2	−4		
		+3	
−1	−1		−2
		+1	
0	0		2
		−1	
+1	−1		2
		3	
2	4		2
		5	
3	9		2
		7	
4	16		−2
		−9	
+5	−25		

And comparing with Example 1, it is seen that the effect is to change the signs of all the difference. The second differences being negative, show that the curve has a maximum point and that it is concave to the axis of x (that is concave to a line below the curve); and graphically, Fig. 1, it has been revolved round the axis of X 180° and lies wholly below it. The effect upon the Finite Differences is also seen. For $x = +3$ u becomes − 9, and the first difference (below the line as usual,) is − 7.

9. *A constant connected with a variable by the sign plus or minus disappears in differentiation,* but the curve is moved along the axis of U. In the general equation (9), let $a = 2$ a constant, thus we have

$$\left. \begin{aligned} u &= 2 + x^2 \\[4pt] \frac{du}{dx} &= 2x \end{aligned} \right\} \qquad (15)$$

With this equation form the finite differences as in Example 2. It is seen that although the column u is not the same as in Ex-

EXAMPLE 2, $u = 2 + x^2$ (15)

x	u	Δ_1	Δ_2
−5	+27		
		−9	
4	18		+2
		7	
3	11		2
		5	
2	6		2
		3	
−1	3		2
		−1	
0	2		2
		+1	
+1	3		2
		3	
2	6		+2
		5	
+3	+11		

ample 1, yet the differences are identical, since the constant cancels out in the subtraction. In other words we have a portion of the example as follows:

$$x = -5, \quad u = +25 + 2$$
$$x = -4, \quad u = +16 + 2$$
$$x = -3, \quad u = + 9 + 2$$

when u is seen to be composed of two terms the first being identical with Example 1, and the other a constant. The first term gives of course the same differences as in Example 1 but the second term has no differences. That is a constant term has no differential and disappears in differentiation as it does in Finite Differences. If we plot the numbers in Example 2 on Fig. 1, we find that it is similar to that figure, but raised two units along the axis of U or what is the same thing it will be the curve of Example 1 if the axis of X should be drawn through the point P. The effect of this independent constant is thus not to alter the curve itself, but to place it differently upon the axes.

10.   We see also that when integrating we must always affix the letter C to the result to allow for a constant that may have disappeared in differentiating.

11.   *Effect of a constant connected with the function of the variable.* The curve moved along the axis of X. In the general equation 9, let $b = +2$

Then

$$\left. \begin{aligned} u &= (x + 2)^2 = x^2 + 4x + 4 \\ \frac{du}{dx} &= 2x + 4 \end{aligned} \right\} \qquad (16)$$

This equation with its differences is shown in Example 3, where u is seen to differ from Example 1 by a variable quantity, but the

EXAMPLE 3, $u = (2 + x)^2$ (16)

x	u	Δ_1	Δ_2
−5	+9		
		−5	
4	4		+2
		3	
3	+1		2
		−1	
2	0		2
		+1	
−1	+1		2
		3	
0	4		2
		5	
+1	9		+2
		+7	
+2	+16		

differences are still the same indicating the same curve as before;

but still differently placed upon the axes, that is, moved along the axis of X, two units.

12. *Explanation of two forms of an equation resulting from Integration, differing by a constant.* If we Integrate equation (16) viz.

$$\frac{du}{dx} = 2x + 4$$

we have

$$u = \int (2x + 4) \, dx = x^2 + 4x + C \qquad (17)$$

We cannot determine the value of the constant C from this equation alone, for if $x = 0$, $C = 0$. It is seen that the constant 4 moves the curve 4 units along the axis of U and the constant 2 also moves it 2 units along the axis of X. Fig. 1. The student may form the differences and test this. We can, however, integrate this equation in another way by factoring out the constant 2, thus

$$u = \int (2x + 4) = \int (x + 2) 2dx = (x + 2)^2 + C \qquad (18)$$

If $x = 0$, $C = -4$ which reduces this equation to the previous form; but if C is taken as zero (for the constants are generally arbitrary) we have the original equation (16). It is thus seen that integration may teach us something, by giving us a form of equation we did not previously know. And moreover the works on the Calculus do not generally explain this point sufficiently,—why a figure or quantity may be summarily dropped or how a constant mysteriously appears; But when we know that these quantities refer only to the position of the curve upon the coördinate axes, and that the position of the axes is arbitrary, then the matter becomes clear at once.

13. *A constant factor of the variable appears in the differences.* All the differences are affected proportionally. The curve is spread out or contracted.

In the general equation 9 let $c = \dfrac{1}{2}$. Thus

$$\left. \begin{aligned} u &= \frac{1}{2} x^2 \\ \frac{du}{dx} &= \frac{1}{2} 2x = x \\ \frac{d^2u}{dx^2} &= 1 \end{aligned} \right\} \qquad (19)$$

x	u	$\triangle_1$	$\triangle_2$
		EXAMPLE 4. $u = \tfrac{1}{2}x^2$. (19.)	
−4	+8.0		
		−3.5	
3	4.5		+1.0
		2.5	
2	2.0		1.0
		1.5	
−1	0.5		1.0
		−0.5	
0	0.0		1.0
		+0.5	
+1	0.5		1.0
		1.5	
2	2.0		1.0
		2.5	
3	4.5		+1.0
		+3.5	
+4	+8.0		

The differences of this equation are given in Example 4. The effect of this constant factor is seen to be, that all the differences are one half of the corresponding values in Example 1; that is in the words of the calculus "a constant factor appears in the differentials." (Courteney) The curve of this last equation is shown in Fig. 1 by a series of dots upon the ordinates. The effect is to spread out the curve, or flatten it toward the axis of X. If the constant factor had not been a fraction, but an integer 2, 3, etc., the curve would have been compressed,—the branches drawn together.

14. *A change in the value of the independent variable, alters the interval of the computed values.* We will resume equations 10 and 11 of the first example namely:

$$\left. \begin{aligned} u &= x^2 \\ \frac{du}{dx} &= 2x \\ \frac{d^2u}{dx^2} &= 2 \end{aligned} \right\} \qquad (20)$$

We also have

As the value of dx is arbitrary, it is usually as a matter of simplicity taken as unity; or in other words whatever the actual interval may be it is considered as a unit. This unit may be one day or one hour or a period of 20 days, etc. When interpolating a function the interval of computed dates is always considered as a unit. In this example, however, we will take this interval as one half, that is, $dx = \dfrac{1}{2}$.

Then the above equations become

$$\left. \begin{aligned} du &= 2xdx &= 2x \cdot \frac{1}{2} &= x \\ d^2u &= 2dx^2 &= 2 \cdot \left(\frac{1}{2}\right)^2 &= \tfrac{1}{2} \end{aligned} \right\} \qquad (21)$$

These equations are shown in Example 5.

EXAMPLE 5. EQUATION (21).

$$u = x^2 \qquad du = \frac{1}{2}.$$

x	u	Δ_1	Δ_2
−2	+4.00		
		−1.75	
1.5	2.25		+0.50
		1.25	
1.0	1.00.		+0.50
		0.75	
−0.5	0.25		0.50
		−0.25	
0.0	0.00		0.50
		+0 25	
+0.5	0.25		0.50
		0.75	
1.0	1.00		0.50
		1.25	
1.5	2.25		+0.50
		1.75	
+2.0	+4.00		

If we should take the interval as one-fourth, then we should
have

$$\left.\begin{aligned}
\frac{du}{dx} &= 2x\,dx = 2\,x \cdot \frac{1}{4} = \frac{1}{2}\,x \\[4pt]
\frac{d^2u}{dx^2} &= 2dx^2 = 2 \cdot \frac{1}{16} = \frac{1}{8}
\end{aligned}\right\} \tag{22}$$

15. It is seen from these equations that by diminishing the interval of the computed dates that the first difference is diminished
$\frac{1}{n}$ the second differences $\left(\dfrac{1}{n}\right)^2$ the third differences $\left(\dfrac{1}{n}\right)^3$ and so on.

In any computation therefore if we find there are higher differences that are inconveniently large for interpolation or other
purposes we can cause them to become less or practically to
vanish by diminishing the interval of the computed quantities.

16. *Particular values of an equation.* Maxima and Minima.
The rule in the calculus for this is to differentiate and place the
first differential coefficient equal to zero, and solve the equation
with respect to x. If x results a finite value or zero it indicates
one of these two. This value of x substituted in the original
equation, gives its maximum or minimum value. To ascertain
which one it is, differentiate a second time, and if the value of x
found above makes the second differential coefficient positive, the
point is a minimum, but if the sign results negative, the point is
a maximum.

To illustrate this we will take equation (11) of Example 1,
(for we have not yet exhausted this little equation.)

$$\left.\begin{aligned}
u &= x^2 \\[4pt]
\frac{du}{dx} &= 2x = 0 \quad \text{Then } x = 0 \\[4pt]
\frac{d^2u}{dx^2} &= +2 \qquad \text{positive value}
\end{aligned}\right\} \tag{23}$$

The first differential coefficient when placed equal to zero and solved gives $x = 0$, and this substituted in the first of these equations gives $u = 0$.

The second differential coefficient has the positive sign which shows that the value $u = 0$ is a minimum.

This same process can be made use of with the differences in Example 1. We here look for a point of the curve which is parallel to the axis of X because $\dfrac{du}{dx}$ being the tangent of the angle which the curve makes with the axis of X, if there is a minimum point the curve after descending turns and then ascends, and the lowest point is when the curve is parallel to the axis of X. Its tangent line being parallel, the angle must be zero and the trigonometrical tangent is zero or the first difference $\Delta_1 = 0$.

We therefore examine the column of 1st Differences for the value 0 opposite which we have the values of u and x. In some equations, the curve may approach the axis of X and become parallel to it but yet contain no maximum or minimum, $\dfrac{d^2u}{dx^2}$ being 0 is neither $+$ nor $-$. This is the case with the cubical parabola given by the equation $u = x^3$. The origin is a point of inflexion.

17. *Points of Inflexion.* It was remarked in Article 7 that the curve Fig. 1 was convex to the axis of X in which case $\dfrac{d^2u}{dx^2}$ is positive. When the curve is concave to the axis $\dfrac{d^2u}{dx^2}$ is negative. At the point of inflexion therefore $\dfrac{d^2u}{dx^2}$ must change its sign, which it cannot do unless it becomes 0 or ∞. Hence these values characterize a point of inflexion.

$$\frac{d^2u}{dx^2} = 0 \qquad \text{or} \qquad \frac{d^2u}{dx^2} = \infty \tag{24}$$

The example in Article 19 $u = x^5$ shows a point of inflexion when $x = 0$. A simpler example is given in the cubical parabola $u = x^3$ which may be computed, differenced, and plotted, by the student.

18. *Cusps.* These are indicated according to the Calculus by $\dfrac{du}{dx}$ having two equal and real values. Thus in the semi-cubical parabola,

$$\left. \begin{array}{l} u^2 = x^3 \\ u = \sqrt{x^3} \end{array} \right\} \tag{25}$$

Solving this equation for various values of x we have the following values and differences:

x	u	Δ_1	Δ_2	Δ_3	Δ_4
-2					
		0.000			
-1			0.000		
		0.000		∓1.000	
0	0.000		∓1.000		±1.172
		∓1.000		±0.172	
1	$\mp1\,000$		0.828		±0.116
		1.828		0.288	
2	2.828		0.540		∓0.184
		2.368		0.104	
3	5.196		0.436		∓0.044
		2.804		±0.060	
4	8.000		∓0.376		
		∓3.180			
5	∓11.180				

There are no real values for the negative values of x, and for $x = 0$ the first real value x = 0 appears; for each positive value of x we have two real and equal values with contrary signs,—in fact two curves. Hence $u = 0$ is a cusp-point. The form of the curve, the reader can doubtless find in any work on the Calculus. Δ_2 having the double sign the value $u = 0$ is a maximum for one branch and a minimum for the other.

19. *The Distinction between a Differential and a Difference rigorously shown.* Professor Chauvenet in his Spherical and Practical Astronomy has deduced a series of formulae for transforming a series of Finite Differences into Differential coefficients. These formulae are similar to the usual formulae for interpolation, both being derived from the algebraic formula for the sum of the series. In the present formulae in order to interpolate for values lying in a horizontal line with the primitive, the even differences, and the mean of the odd differences are employed; but in the general formula for interpolation, where the value lies between the given primitive and the next following, the odd differences and the mean of the even are employed.

These formulae which may also be found in Watson's *Theoretical Astronomy* are as follows,—changing Chauvenet's notation slightly to conform to that of the present work.*

$$
\left.
\begin{aligned}
\frac{du}{dx} &= \frac{1}{w}\left(\frac{\Sigma\Delta_1}{2} - \frac{1}{6}\,\frac{\Sigma\Delta_3}{2} + \frac{1}{30}\,\frac{\Sigma\Delta_5}{2} - \text{etc.} \right) \\[4pt]
\frac{d^2u}{dx^2} &= \frac{1}{w^2}\left(\Delta_2 - \frac{1}{12}\,\Delta_4 + \text{etc.} \right) \\[4pt]
\frac{d^3u}{dx^3} &= \frac{1}{w^3}\left(\frac{\Sigma\Delta_3}{2} - \frac{1}{4}\,\frac{\Sigma\Delta_5}{2} + \text{etc.} \right) \\[4pt]
\frac{d^4u}{dx^4} &= \frac{1}{w^4}\left(\Delta_4 - \text{etc.} \right) \\[4pt]
\frac{d^5u}{dx^5} &= \frac{1}{w^5}\left(\frac{\Sigma\Delta_5}{2} - \text{etc.} \right)
\end{aligned}
\right\} \qquad (26)
$$

---

* The author has employed differences extensively in computations of the planets for the Nautical Almanac, U. S. Naval Observatory. The hourly motions printed in the Nautical Almanac, and the aberration are computed by means of the first equation of formula (26). The formulae are also used for correcting the elements of orbit of a planet from three or more observations. In this way, more than twenty-five years ago, he discovered this method of explaining the Calculus.

In these equations the notation $\dfrac{\Sigma\Delta}{2}$ denotes the mean of the adjacent odd differences, lying above and below the line D in Example 6. The factor w is used if we wish to reduce the differential to a lesser interval than that of the tabulated values. As we here use the formulae it is unity, and neglected.

20. In this article we will assume the equation

$$u = x^5 \tag{27}$$

with which we form the following tabulated values with their differences, Example 6 as follows:

EXAMPLE 6. $u = x^5$, EQUATION 27.

x	u	Δ_1	Δ_2	Δ_3	Δ_4	Δ_5	
−3	− 243						
		+ 211					
−2	−32		− 180				
		31		+ 150			
−1	− 1		- 30		−120		
		+		30		+120	
0	0		0		0		
		+		30		120	
+1	+ 1		+ 30		+120		
		31		150		120	
2	32		180		240		
		211		390		120	
3	243		570		360		D
		781		750		120	
4	1024		1320		480		
		2101		1230		120	
5	3125		2550		+600		
		4651		+1830		+120	
6	7776		+4380				F
		+9031					
7	+16807						

For the numerical values to be used we assume

$$x = + 3 \tag{28}$$

and for this value the differential coefficients lie in the horizontal line from 3^5 to D, while the Finite Differences lie in the diagonal from 3^5 to F.

The differential coefficients will now be formed, and their values for $x = + 3$ computed, as follows:

$$\left.\begin{aligned}
\frac{du}{dx} &= 5x^4, &\text{and when } x = 3 \quad &= 405\\[4pt]
\frac{d^2u}{dx^2} &= 20x^3, & &= 540\\[4pt]
\frac{d^3u}{dx^3} &= 60x^2 & &= 540\\[4pt]
\frac{d^4u}{dx^4} &= 120x, & &= 360\\[4pt]
\frac{d^5u}{dx^5} &= 120, & &= 120
\end{aligned}\right\} \tag{29}$$

Now substituting in equation (26) the mean of the odd differences, and the values of the even differences lying along the horizontal line D in Example 6, we have

$$\frac{du}{dx} = \frac{992}{2} - \frac{1}{6}\cdot\frac{1140}{2} + \frac{1}{30}\cdot\frac{240}{2} = 496 - 95 + 4 = 405$$

$$\frac{d^2u}{dx^2} = 570 - \frac{1}{12}\,360 \qquad = 570 - 30 \qquad = 540$$

$$\frac{d^3u}{dx^3} = \frac{1140}{2} - \frac{1}{4}\cdot\frac{240}{2} \qquad = 570 - 30 \qquad = 540 \quad\Big\} \quad (30)$$

$$\frac{d^4u}{dx^4} = 360 \qquad\qquad\qquad\qquad\qquad\qquad = 360$$

$$\frac{d^5u}{dx^5} = 120 \qquad\qquad\qquad\qquad\qquad\qquad = 120$$

which values agree with the differential coefficients found above in equation 29, by differentiation.

21.   It is further and clearly seen that one distinction between a differential coefficient and a Finite Difference is one of POSITION in the scheme of tabulated Finite Differences. And a Differential Coefficient of any order may be correctly defined as that certain interpolated value of a series of tabulated Finite Differences of the same order, which lies in a horizontal line with its primitive function; while the Finite Differences are those values obtained by subtraction which lie in the downward diagonal from the same primitive function.

22.   *Further criticisms on the Method by Limits.* We see moreover from the first equation of 29 that when applied to a function of the second power there is but one term.

$$\frac{du}{xd} = \frac{1}{2}\,\Sigma\,\Delta_1 = \begin{cases} \Delta_1\,(\text{upper value}) + \tfrac{1}{2}\,\Delta_2 \\ \Delta_1\,(\text{lower value}) - \tfrac{1}{2}\,\Delta_2 \end{cases} \qquad (31)$$

which by the differences of example 1 when x = 3 becomes

$$\frac{du}{dx} = \Delta_1 - \frac{1}{2}\,\Delta_2 = 7 - 1 = 6$$

Again

$$u = x^2 \qquad \frac{du}{dx} = 2x, \text{ (when } x = 3) = 6$$

We now discover what becomes of the term h in equation   (4)

$$u_1 - u = 2xh + h^2$$

in which h must be taken equal to unity to correspond with the interval in Example 1. It does not "disappear" by becoming less and less, but is controlled or cancelled by the term $\dfrac{1}{2}\,\Delta_2$ in equation (26) which is 1 in equations of the second degree, (provided the coefficient of x in the primitive equation is unity.)

23.   We are now prepared to say that in such equations as (7)

which we have been considering, that for any given value of x both $u_1 - u$ and $2x$ are constants, (with coefficients however,) which becomes apparent by examining the changes which take place while h is supposed to decrease without limit. We will examine both equations (4) and (7) as follows:

Equation (4).   Equation (7).

$$u_1 - u = 2xh + h^2 \qquad\qquad \frac{u_1 - u}{h} = 2x + h$$

$$\text{When } x = 1, \quad u_1 - u = 2x + 1 \qquad\qquad (u_1 - u) = 2x + 1$$

$$= \frac{1}{2}, \quad u_1 - u = \frac{2x}{2} + \frac{1}{4} \qquad\qquad 2(u_1 - u) = 2x + \frac{1}{2}$$

$$= \frac{1}{4}, \quad u_1 - u = \frac{2x}{4} + \frac{1}{16} \qquad\qquad 4(u_1 - u) = 2x + \frac{1}{4}$$

$$= \frac{1}{8}, \quad u_1 - u = \frac{2x}{8} + \frac{1}{64} \qquad\qquad 8(u_1 - u) = 2x + \frac{1}{8}$$

$$\text{Limit,} \quad 0, \quad u_1 - u = 0 + 0 \qquad\qquad \infty(u_1 - u) = 2x + 0.$$

These equations are convertible to one another as they should be; in the first the quantity $2x$ does not remain to reach the limit as fondly hoped in this method; but becomes equal to zero; the term $(u_1 - u)$ also becomes equal to zero and there is nothing left but the primitive equation. This is the correct and legitimate effect of diminishing the value of h. In the other equation although the quantity $2x$ remains yet the coefficient of the left member becomes infinite, and at the limit $(u_1 - u)$ takes the indeterminate form $\dfrac{2x}{\infty}$; an inconsistency arising from neglecting the fundamental principle of Finite Differences, that h must be a constant.

24. In Haddon's "Examples in the Differential Calculus," Weales Series London, the above mentioned inconsistencies are very clearly shown. Assuming the equation $u = x^3$ the author proceeds, "$\dfrac{u_1 - u}{h} = 3x^2 + 3xh + h^2 =$ Ratio of increment of function to increment of variable. Now the first term of this expression for the ratio being $3x^2$, it is obvious that h may undergo any change of value whatever, without affecting this first term. Let h then continually decrease in value until it is $= 0$."

May it? Most assuredly it may; but this sophistry keeps out of sight that the first member becomes infinite from which nothing can then be proved.

We see that in the first member of all these similar equations, that $(u_1 - u)$ does not suffer much decrease in value. In fact it cannot decrease smaller than the first term of the second member, while its denominator h decreases without limit.

There seems to be also another peculiarity in these equations. They start with x as a variable receiving the increment h, but when $(u_1 - u)$ is reached x seems to be regarded as a constant with h a variable!

The true nature of the change which this method by limits endeavors to explain is shown in Equations (26) to (30) where it is seen that all the terms of the higher differences combine in certain proportions by interpolation and are numerically added to or subtracted from the first term (which remains unchanged) and thus make the change in the first member of the equation, while this new numerical value is still denoted by the quantity $3x^2$ in the present equations and $2x$ in those on the previous pages. This is an intricate point and sophistry can make much out of it. In one sense $3x^2$ is constant and in another sense it has changed its numerical value. The numerical value depends upon whether we regard $3x^2$ as a term of a Finite Difference or a Differential Coefficient. How easy to slide from one to the other! not knowing or suppressing the fact that the numerical values are different.

Finally. If we have a quantity x and add to it another quantity h and let h diminish until it becomes zero, what in the name of common sense have we left but the original quantity?

25. *The reverse problem. Finite Differences derived from Differential Coefficients.* Professor George Boole has given in his Calculus of Finite Differences* the following formula which is the fundamental relation between finite differences and differential coefficients:

$$\triangle^n u = \frac{d^n u}{dx^n} + \frac{\triangle^n 0^{n+1}}{1.2.(n+1)} \cdot \frac{\triangle^{n+1} u}{dx^{n+1}} \left. + \frac{\triangle^n 0^{n+2}}{1.2.(n+2)} \cdot \frac{d^{n+2} u}{dx^{n+2}} + \text{etc.} \right\} \quad (32A)$$

in which the coefficients are complicated quantities,—the numerators being computed by the expression

$$\triangle^n 0^m = n^m - n(n-1)^m + \frac{n(n-1)(n-2)^m}{1.2} - \frac{n(n-1)(n-2)(n-3)^m}{1.2.3} + \text{etc.} \quad (32B)$$

I understand that in some editions of Boole's work the numerators have been computed and tabulated. Applied to the differentials these formulae become:

---

* Macmillan & Co., London, 1872.

$$\Delta_1 = \frac{du}{dx} + \frac{1}{2}\,\frac{d^2u}{dx^2} + \frac{1}{6}\,\frac{d^3u}{dx^3} + \frac{1}{24}\,\frac{d^4u}{dx^4} + \frac{1}{120}\,\frac{d^5u}{dx^5}$$

$$\Delta_2 = \frac{d^2u}{dx^2} + \frac{d^3u}{dx^3} + \frac{7}{12}\,\frac{d^4u}{dx^4} + \frac{1}{4}\,\frac{d^5u}{dx^5}$$

$$\Delta_3 = \frac{d^3u}{dx^3} + \frac{3}{2}\,\frac{d^4u}{dx^4} + \frac{5}{4}\,\frac{d^5u}{dx^5}$$

$$\Delta_4 = \frac{d^4u}{dx^4} + 2\,\frac{d^5u}{dx^5}$$

$$\Delta_5 = \frac{d^5u}{dx^5}$$

$$(33)$$

Inserting the values of the differential coefficients from Equation (30)

$$
\begin{aligned}
\Delta_1 &= 405 + 270 + 90 + 15 + 1 = 781 \\
\Delta_2 &= 540 + 540 + 210 + 30 \quad\; = 1320 \\
\Delta_3 &= 540 + 540 + 150 + \quad\;\; = 1230 \\
\Delta_4 &= 360 + 240 \qquad\qquad\quad\; = 600 \\
\Delta_5 &= 120 \qquad\qquad\qquad\qquad = 120
\end{aligned}
\qquad (34)
$$

These differences agree with those in Example 6 lying on the diagonal line ending at F.

26.   According to Boole the equation for the several differences in terms of the Differential coefficients, equation (32) is the fundamental relation between Differences and Differentials. From equation (33) it is again seen that the first differential coefficient is not the same as the First Difference which is perhaps the chief fallacy in the usual explanation of the calculus.

The only exception to this is that the nth Differential coefficient is always equal to the nth Difference which is a constant in both finite difference and differentials.

27.   *Inversion of the Series*, in Example 6, Article 20.

It will be interesting to note what effect this inversion has upon the results of the two formulae in Articles 19 and 25. This is equivalent to taking equation 27 with the negative sign.

The Tabular differences then are as follows:

x	u	Δ_1	Δ_2	Δ_3	Δ_4	Δ_5	
4	+1024		+1320		+480		
		−781		−750		−120	
3	243		570		360		D'
		211		390		120	
2	32		180		240		
		31		150		120	
1	1		30		+120		
				− 30		−120	
0	+ 0		+ 0		+ 0		F

The Differential Coefficients still lie in the horizontal line 3 — D' while the Finite Differences are again in the downward diagonal 3 — F' which now includes quite a different set of numbers from the previous table. Finite differences thus change when a . series is inverted. Changes of signs are also noted above.

Agreeing numerically with those previously found in the same manner and with the change of signs the inversion of the series necessitates, and also lying in the horizontal line of the tabulated differences.

By formula 33 we have the Finite Differences from the Differential Coefficients, employing those just found.

$$\begin{aligned}
\triangle_1 &= -405 + 270 - 90 + 15 - 1 = -496 + 285 = -211 \\
\triangle_2 &= +540 - 540 + 210 - 30 \qquad\quad = +750 - 570 = +180 \\
\triangle_3 &= -540 + 540 - 150 \qquad\qquad\qquad\qquad\quad = -150 \\
\triangle_4 &= +360 - 240 \qquad\qquad\qquad\qquad\qquad\quad = +120 \\
\triangle_5 &= -120 \qquad\qquad\qquad\qquad\qquad\qquad\quad = -120
\end{aligned} \tag{36}$$

Corresponding exactly with the new values of Finite Differences, lying in the diagonal line 3-F'. These two diagonal lines of Finite Differences are symmetrically disposed above and below the horizontal line of Differential Coefficients.

28. *Concluding Remarks on the Method by Limits.* The foregoing pages following example 6 Articles 19-20 show that the differential coefficients depend upon the interval of the argument x of finite differences being taken as unity; whatever the actual interval may be. We may, however, decrease the *actual* interval (Art. 15) while still regarding it as a unit, or even consider it infinitely small as customary in investigations. The author does not wish to be considered as holding that a differential must be unity or a large quantity. His object being only to prove that h in equations 2, 3, 4, 5 must be a unit and cannot be considered as a variable decreasing without limit.

Finally, the author asks if the method by limits can show the second differential coefficient? Can it be derived by another infinitely small quantity k? Does its derivation follow the same law as the first? It would be illogical to infer that it does, for that is begging the question—the very point we wish to know.

The method by Limits regards a differential coefficient as a *ratio* to which objection has been made; but finite differences being formed by subtraction, the differential coefficient derived from them is not a ratio.

9 789391 270001